# This Is How I Help!

## *How Little Ones Can Help Their Friends with Autism*

BY WENDI SOBELMAN

ILLUSTRATED BY MIKE MOTZ

Illustrated by Mike Motz
Edited by Pam Halter

ISBN 978-1-938796-94-4 paperback
ISBN 978-1-938796-93-7 hardback
ISBN 978-1-938796-95-1 ebook

Library of Congress Control Number: 2021913977

SAN 920-380X
ISNI 0000 0000 5048 9968
Ages 2-7

Children's Fiction/Education

Fruitbearer Kids
Published by Fruitbearer Publishing LLC
P.O. Box 777, Georgetown, DE 19947
302.856.6649 • FAX 302.856.7742
www.fruitbearer.com • info@fruitbearer.com



Printed in the United States of America

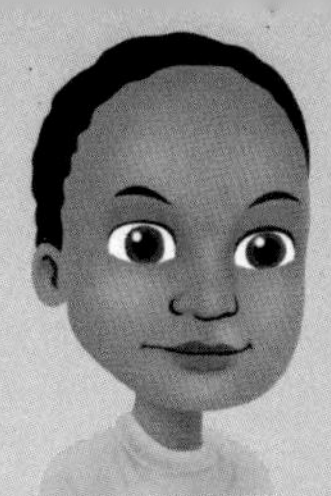

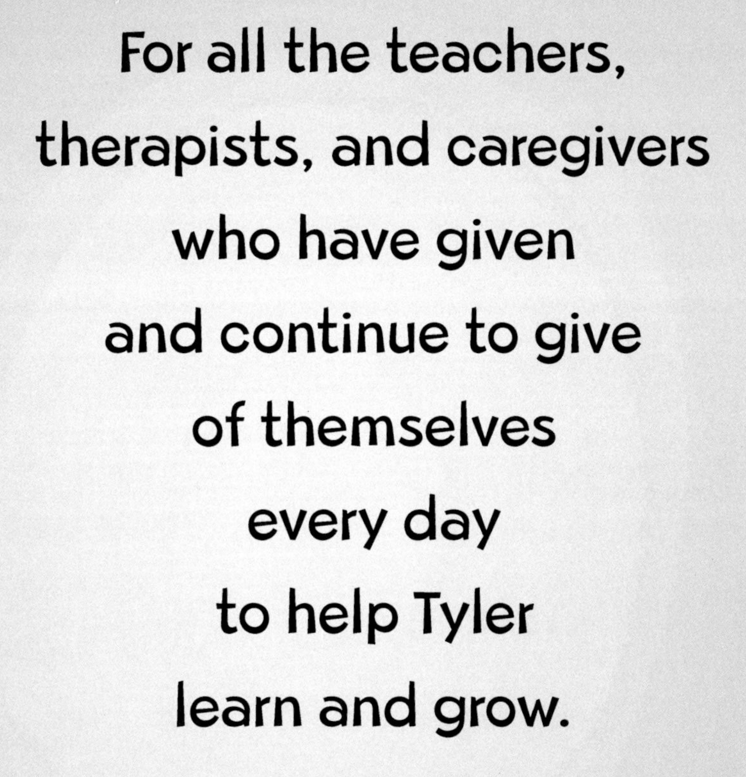

For all the teachers,
therapists, and caregivers
who have given
and continue to give
of themselves
every day
to help Tyler
learn and grow.

---

You are very special people.

## ACKNOWLEDGMENTS

Thank you to my husband, Howard,
for all of your advice
and for being the most wonderful
hands-on dad there is.

Thanks also to my parents,
siblings, extended family, and friends
for always supporting me and my family unit
as we navigate through the world of autism.

A special thank you to my children,
Jacob, Reanna, and Tyler.
You were the inspirations for this book.

Thank you to Mike Motz for the beautiful illustrations.

I would also like to thank everyone over at Fruitbearer Kids
for believing in this project and for their professional guidance.

# This Book Will

Serve as a springboard for discussion for teachers, parents, or anyone in a position to discuss autism with a youngster.

Be a useful tool for parents and teachers to read to or with children ages 2-7 to benefit the classmates, friends, siblings, and relatives of children with autism.

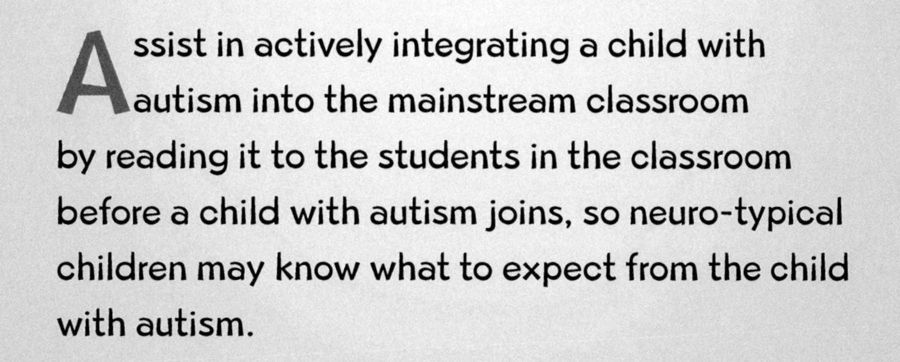

Assist in actively integrating a child with autism into the mainstream classroom by reading it to the students in the classroom before a child with autism joins, so neuro-typical children may know what to expect from the child with autism.

Hi, my name is Jacob, and I am learning about the word "help." My teacher says we have a new student starting school today. His name is Tyler. My teacher says he acts a little differently from the rest of the class, but he does not look any different to me. I want to help the new student.

My teacher says he has something called autism (ah-tiz-um). I do not know what that means. The teacher says we should help Tyler feel good in the classroom. I want Tyler to be my new friend. *This is how I help.*

Tyler rides the school bus every day. He is lucky because he always has a grown-up with him to keep him safe. I make sure he sees a friendly face when he gets off the bus, so I say, "Hi, Tyler. I am your friend Jacob." *This is how I help.*

Tyler has not learned how to talk yet, but he found many ways to tell us what he wants. He can make different sounds and noises. When he makes noises and flaps his hands in the air, I know he is either happy and excited or upset.

His noises do not scare me, so I do not stare at him or run away. When I see Tyler is happy, it makes me happy, too. If his noises do not sound happy, I will let the teacher know. *This is how I help.*

Tyler found a different way to talk without using his voice. He moves his hands and taps his body when he wants something. It is called sign-language. When Tyler touches his cheek with his finger, he wants candy. When he touches his fingers on both hands together, he wants more.

If I am doing a puzzle with Tyler and he gives me the sign for more, then I give him another puzzle piece. By watching Tyler, I am learning sign-language, too! *This is how I help.*

Tyler is lucky. He gets to use his very own iPad at school that talks for him. When he touches a picture on the screen, the iPad speaks the name of the picture.

Tyler is great at spelling. He can spell lots of words. I only know how to spell a little. When Tyler types the word crayon on his iPad, the iPad says "crayon." I can then get a crayon for him. *This is how I help.*

Tyler likes to read a lot and play by himself. All of his favorite toys play music or teach letters and numbers. He feels good when he pushes the same button over and over again and hears the same sound. I guess that is how he got to be so smart. I do not want him to feel lonely, so I sit next to him and play my own game. *This is how I help.*

Tyler likes to chew on pencils, crayons, and toys because it makes his mouth feel good. The teacher showed me that he can use a blue rubber tube to chew on instead, so he does not hurt his teeth. *This is how I help.*

Tyler sometimes needs extra help learning. Other teachers come in to play with Tyler and teach him all sorts of things like how to talk, color, and cut out shapes. When we do arts and crafts, I try to help him like the teachers do. *This is how I help.*

When I see Tyler put his hands over his ears, I know the class is too loud for him, and he does not like it. I can try to be quieter or give him his headphones to wear. The headphones make his ears feel better because they make the noise in the room sound softer, but I like that he can still hear me talk to him. *This is how I help.*

When I try to give something to Tyler, he does not always take it from me. It seems like Tyler does not notice that I am standing there because his eyes do not always look at me, but the teacher says he can see me with the sides of his eyes. When I want to get his attention, it can be hard, especially when he is playing with one of his toys.

The teacher says I can stand in front of his eyes and tap him on the shoulder. I did, and he looked straight at me! *This is how I help.*

Sometimes, I do not know what to do for Tyler. He may cry and I do not know why. He often just wants to be left alone, so I will let him be alone.

There is not much I can do when that happens, so I tell the teacher. I will come back to play when he feels better. *This is how I help.*

It makes me feel proud when I can do something to help Tyler. Luckily, he lets me hold his hand when we walk in line so he does not walk away. I am learning that some people with autism may not allow you to hold their hand. I would never force them. *This is how I help.*

If Tyler has a hard time waiting his turn for the slide, I guide him to his place in line, but first I always make sure it is okay with him. If he pushes me away or gets upset when I try to guide him, I get the teacher. *This is how I help.*

I do not fully understand what autism is or why Tyler does some things differently than me, but that is okay. We all cannot be the same. I guess we all need help in different ways. I am glad to be Tyler's new friend. *This is how I help . . .*

*. . . and how*
*Tyler helps me!*

# Let's Talk About Autism

Think about someone you know who is not like you.

- **How did you feel about being with them?**
- **Now that you have learned about Tyler, how will you feel about being with someone not like you?**

Some children with autism talk a lot! They can talk about one thing specifically, like dinosaurs, and tell you all the information you ever wanted to know about dinosaurs. While some children with autism can repeat what you say, others do not speak at all. That is why they use sign language or an electronic device that speaks for them.

- **What is another way you can talk without using words?**

Some children with autism like things that repeat. They may hit a button that makes a sound over and over again so they can hear the same sound. Some children with autism do that because they find it soothing and calming.

- **Is there something that you like to do that makes you feel calm?**

Some children with autism may feel things too much, like Tyler who gets upset when he hears certain noises because they sound extra loud. Some children may feel things too little and need something to help provide extra feeling, such as when Tyler uses the rubber chewy tube to feel the sensations in his mouth.

- **Do you occasionally feel things too much or too little?**

Not all children with autism look or act the same. For example, some flap their hands when they are excited, while others may make sounds with their mouths.

- **How do you act when you are excited?**

Jacob was very respectful of Tyler's differences when helping him.

- **What do you think would have happened to Tyler if no one helped him?**
- **What would you do if you didn't know how to help?**

# MEET THE AUTHOR

*Photography by Tolga Tuncay*

Wendi Sobelman is a former educator with a Master of Arts degree in Counseling from Ottawa University and an undergraduate degree from the University of Arizona. Wendi is a mother of triplets, including a son with autism who is currently a young adult. Past publications include articles on autism and articles about having triplets which were featured in various national magazines. In 2019, Wendi was featured on an episode of the TV show "Catalyst" regarding aging with autism. Wendi has been involved with the Southwest Autism Research & Resource Center (SARRC), the Gesher Disability Resources Board of Directors, and other local organizations serving those with disabilities. Wendi also previously served on the Board of Directors for her local chapter of the National Charity League. Wendi lives in Scottsdale, AZ with her husband, three children, and their dog Wilson. For more information about Wendi and her work, visit www.facebook.com/WendiSobelmanhelpsautism.

# MEET THE ILLUSTRATOR

For more than eighteen years, Mike Motz and his company of fellow artists have created illustrations for over 500 children's books, one of them being this extraordinary book you're enjoying right now. Mike loves working with both first-time and experienced authors to make their dream of bringing their children's book to life a reality. For more information about Mike and his work, please visit www.mikemotz.com.

# Autism Facts & Resources

In the United States, one in fifty-four children are diagnosed with autism spectrum disorder (ASD), making it the most prevalent childhood developmental disorder in the U.S.[1] Autism spectrum disorder is a developmental disorder that affects communication and behavior. ASD is characterized by social impairments, communication difficulties, and restricted, repetitive and stereotyped patterns of behavior.[2]

As a whole, children with autism fail to develop appropriate socialization. They have disturbances in speech, language, and communication. Children with autism tend to have abnormal responses to sensory stimuli either through overreacting or underreacting. They generally have abnormal relationships to objects and events. Children with autism tend to experience developmental delays and differences, and their rate of development and sequence of development may be unusual. Autism usually presents in the first three years of life, affecting boys four times more than girls. Associated problems include hyperactivity, self-injurious behavior, sleeplessness, attention difficulties, eating disorders, and seizures.[3]

While some children with autism develop some normal and even advanced skills, they exhibit a wide range of behavioral deficiencies and excesses.[4] No two autistic children present exactly the same symptoms in the same way. Early intensive behavioral intervention therapies, though not a cure, can make a significant difference in the life of a child with autism. Many children with autism can learn and live productive lives.

To learn more about autism and how you can help, please contact:

**Autism Speaks**
1 East 33rd St., 4th Floor
New York, New York 10016
(888) 288-4762
www.Autismspeaks.org
help@autismspeaks.org

**Autism Society of America** (ASA)
6110 Executive Boulevard Suite 305
Rockville, MD 20814
(800) 3-AUTISM: call for the ASA chapter nearest you
www.autism-society.org

**Southwest Autism Research & Resource Center** (SARRC)
300 N. 18th St.
Phoenix, AZ 85006
(602) 340-8717
www.autismcenter.org
email: help@autismcenter.org

---

1 Center for Disease Control (2020)
2 Staff. (2020). *Southwest Autism Research & Resource Center* (on-line). Phoenix, AZ
3 Powers, M.D., Psy. D. (Ed.). (2000). What is Autism?, *Children with Autism: A Parent's Guide* (2nd ed.) (pp. 1-9). Bethesda, MD: Woodbine House.
4 Staff. (2000, July) What is autism? *Families for Early Autism Treatment (FEAT)* {on-line}. Portland, Oregon.

# Order Info

*This Is How I Help*

Available from Amazon or your favorite bookseller.
For autographed books
or to schedule speaking engagements, visit
www.facebook.com/WendiSobelmanhelpsautism.

Discounts available for bulk orders and fundraisers
through Fruitbearer Publishing LLC.
www.fruitbearer.com
info@fruitbearer.com • 302.856.6649
P.O. Box 777, Georgetown, DE 19947

To find this and other inspirational books
in the Fruitbearer collection,
scan code with your smartphone.

Made in the USA
Monee, IL
17 February 2022